THE ANCIENT ALIEN DOG
(A very brief study on the origin of a species)

Susan Lee Teal

Illustrations by
Ahmad Jordan

This book is a work of fiction, a product of the author's imagination. The names of the author, her brother, those of places and of historical or mythological characters are factual. All others are fictitious. Any resemblance to actual events or locales or persons, living or dead, is coincidental.

The Ancient Alien Dog
Copyright © 2024, All Rights Reserved.

First American Edition July 2024

Manufactured in the United States of America
Text in Times New Roman

ISBN: 9798336885750

Introduction

In early January of 2013, I received word from my brother that I should expect, within a week or two, to have delivered into my possession a unique gift from him. Naturally, I was quite intrigued and so awaited the arrival of the mysterious "offering" with great anticipation!

My brother and I have, in these, our later years, discovered that we have many interests in common. This is a blessing for me, as many of my interests have more often than not been considered a bit "on the fringe" and finding like-minded seekers of truths has always been difficult if not impossible. Having someone as close as a brother to share ideas, research and opinions regarding out-of-the-box subjects is simply wonderful. So, of course, being informed of something unique coming my way delighted me to no end.

James is a retired Special Judge of the District Court in Oklahoma City. He now has more time to spend on his extracurricular interests and activities. That he would choose to use his free time to be involved with the things I find to be of monumental importance is very gratifying.

The day came when I picked up the package from the post office and rushed home with it.

Upon opening the box, I found a card lying on top of the material that was carefully wrapped around the soon-to-be-appreciated contents. In this card, James explained that he had been inspired by my deep interest in ancient aliens and so had involved himself in similar research. His target, however, had focused on ancient alien dogs; hence he now calls himself an "Ancient Alien Dog Theorist."

He went on to say that his research and studies had led him some months ago to a little-known archaeological dig being conducted in Kansas and that a 5,000-year-old structure strongly suggesting its purpose as having been for social imbibing of alcoholic beverages, i.e., a tavern, had already been uncovered. Kansas wasn't too distant and he had the time, so he inquired as to whether or not amateurs would be allowed to participate in the dig. He was pleasantly surprised to learn that he would be welcomed. Beginner's luck was with him. In just a few weeks, while digging through some rare ancient hand-blown glass bottles (one still containing desiccated evidence of what he calls "bad brew"), he found the remains of an ancient dog! He couldn't believe his good fortune! His first real dig and to find exactly what he had hoped for! Without doubt, it was a dog and there seemed little question that it was not of this Earth.

The remains were curiously attached to what looked to be some kind of flat-surfaced metallic rectangular object – oddly similar to a refrigerator door. The contiguous evidence indicated that the dog had died, having fallen victim to consuming bad liquor presumably made by the then-indigenous native population. With permission from the supervising archaeologist, my brother collected the remains and took them home. There, he reconstructed them to the best of his ability, although body and head could not be held together due to missing critical bones. After all this effort, he most generously decided to keep all but the head, which he was herewith bequeathing to me for my analysis and subsequent opinion.

I immediately set to putting together what I know of this matter and wrote the following paper:

IN RESPONSE TO THE QUESTIONS RAISED CONCERNING THE ANCIENT ALIEN DOG SKELETAL REMAINS DISCOVERED BY JUDGE JAMES PADDLEFORD

Not much has been written about this mystifying subject, mainly due to the lack of tangible evidence. Very few skeletal remains and/or other relics dating from the same time period this creature first appeared on Earth have ever been discovered. Even fewer hypotheses concerning this enigmatic entity have been put forward by scientists. It is quite impossible to study a species if specimens are not available for study! Most of what has been written comes from the transcriptions of oral histories handed down by indigenous peoples. Luckily, I possess a talent for psychometry and telepathy as well as extrasensory percipience and have been able, through these methods, to glean much more information about this wonderful creature. You, my dear brother, are uniquely fortunate to have discovered the specimen you sent to me and I thank you for it.

In fact, the remains you found are of an ancient alien, but there is still some question as to the exact species, from where it comes (although I do offer in this paper the strong probability of its origins as per ancestral tales from an African people who have told their history for centuries) and, indeed, its real age. Without doubt, the antecedents of this specimen were here far, far earlier than first speculated. It has been estimated the original members of this race arrived here 450,000 to 500,000 years ago. They were present on Earth, in their true form, for thousands of years before mutations began to appear. They differed physically from the later forms, which is the form you uncovered (and which I would guess is probably around 15,000 years old—not 5,000 as you had suggested), in that they were larger, they had much longer tails and their limbs ended with human-like hands with fingers and feet with toes, rather than paws such as we see today. Adding to their regal stature, heavy manes draped over their heads and onto their shoulders. (It's interesting how millennia later, during the time of Egyptian Pharaohs, the human royals wore headdresses designed to mimic, and perhaps to pay homage to their ancient benefactors. The Nemes, as made famous by King Tutankhamun, is an example.) Their tails were used much the way kangaroos use theirs—to more comfortably stand upright. It is not unreasonable to assume these magnificent beings stood seven-to-ten feet in height, as compared to the four-to-five feet of the primitive primates which were beginning to populate the Earth at that time. The erect posture of these foreign entities facilitated the scientific work they did in their laboratories and the piloting of their intergalactic conveyances.

They came from a very distant planet and were involved in planetary exploration and humanitarian (a term coined millennia after they left Earth) ventures, benefiting the indigenous populations they encountered on their journeys. These interplanetary travelers were higher beings, vastly more advanced intellectually, spiritually and technologically than any living being on Earth. Upon arriving on planet Earth, they saw how one peculiar life form, the aforementioned primate, had evolved thus far, and as it exhibited potential, they determined it could use their assistance. So arrangements were made with their home base and plans were drawn for them to set up a research camp and prepare to stay for as long as it would take (which would be at least tens of thousands of years!) to improve and enlighten these poor creatures.

Several ships brought five twelve-member teams of these beings, and after unloading the essential equipment and supplies, all but one of the ships returned home. The remaining ship would be used far in the future to take the thirty female and thirty male scientists back home when the project was finished. In large letters printed on the bellies of these huge, saucer-shaped ships, identifying insignia could be seen: G.O.D. These letters stood for "Genetics Outreach and Development." Because this is the only clue we have to their identity (they related precious little about themselves—no names or history—only obvious evidence of their work) I have chosen to take license to call these unknown, astronautical scientists GODs.

These GODs didn't want the natives to be unnecessarily troubled or frightened by their superior technology, such as that exhibited by their spaceships, so the remaining ship was housed in a cave, far away from curious eyes and weak minds. Selecting the cave took time, as it was essential that it have a natural protective force field and that it have a large and permanent supply of water. The ship needed constant humidity otherwise it would deteriorate over the length of time expected for this job. The perfect location was finally found; no earth creature witnessed the ship's arrival and it was hidden deep in the cave over a pool of water. The Aliens could then get on with the business of studying and aiding the advancement of the creatures they named "Human," after "humere," as they found this species to often be coated in a rather malodorous fluid we now know as perspiration or sweat, a condition unheard of in GODs.

The naïve, ignorant Earthlings soon accepted the Aliens as other denizens of the land and quickly learned they meant no harm. After overcoming some initial trepidation, caused mainly by the huge size discrepancy between the species, the smaller beings realized they could trust the newcomers.

The Aliens weren't quite as certain about trusting the lumbering, slobbering, squabbling Earthling population, however. Not only were they crude, they could and would bite and scratch!

With much patience and care, the GODs were eventually able to bring these creatures to a point where they could actually be petted, bathed, groomed and taught to walk upright. When the Humans were comfortable with this new life-changing accomplishment, they were taught to do simple tricks, such as shaking hands and fetching sticks. They learned to respond to commands like "Sit," "Lie down," "Come here," and "No." Each time they performed correctly they were given small edible treats. The Humans were thrilled with the attention and were in awe of the GODs' abilities. Even in their very limited, primitive minds, they somehow understood that these superior beings, while being disciplinarians, were also kind and generous, deserving of the Humans' love, respect and gratitude.

Unfortunately, the Humans skewed this love into something different and rather unhealthy. They allowed their inherent laziness to take hold. They gave up the independence the GODs were trying to foster in them and released all responsibility for their behavior back to the GODs. They began to worship the long-tailed Aliens with the hope they could continue just doing tricks for treats. They exhibited an attitude of "who needs enlightenment—just bring on the free food."

The GODs tried to put a stop to this kind of negative behavior, but the Earthlings were not cooperative. They would not stop bowing, kneeling, licking hands and begging for treats. In no time, this escalated into fighting over perceived preferential treatment, the erroneous idea of the GODs liking one Human over another, but favoritism never took place—the GODs remained egalitarian throughout the project. Indeed, teaching equality among individuals was one of the lessons they hoped to impart to the Humans.

Another problem for the scientists was the outrageous scale of breeding that was taking place among these lowly creatures. Their numbers grew much faster than was anticipated, and with these higher numbers, the unrest became ever louder and the perceived competition ever more serious. All other organisms on this planet followed and respected the wisdom of Nature's rules and rhythms. This disrespectful group, if not taught to get in step, could, in the future, be the ruin of the planet's environment. Many of the scientists, while working with the Humans, were bitten, some quite savagely, and they realized that because they were becoming so greatly outnumbered by the potentially vicious crowds, something drastic had to be done. The Humans were rapidly forming factions or packs, all vying for special treatment from the GODs. The scientists had never dealt with such a difficult species before. It was only a matter of time before there would be so many Humans they would overpower the GODs, ruin any in-roads made thus far and put a stop to any further progress—essentially destroying the whole project!

In near desperation, the GODs knew they would have to resort to using their organization's ultimate technological transforming device to help speed evolution in these Humans. By this time, they had already spent several centuries working with these Earthlings, but education was simply not taking speedily enough. With permission from their home planet, they brought out the "DNA-Transfer and Memory-Exchange Mechanism." This device had been used only in simulation runs in the home base laboratory and they knew there could always be inherent dangers in using the machine, especially with a minimally evolved species, but desperate times call for desperate measures. This was, indeed, a very desperate time!

Being the selfless, caring scientists they were, the GODs planned their next move. All but one of them would be volunteers to undergo the transfer/exchange procedure in order to salvage the program, as well as the pitiful Earthlings. Once the volunteers were selected—30 males and 29 females—they set about collecting 1,180 healthy candidates, male and female, from the Human group. This number would allow twenty Humans for each GOD, so the total number of individuals chosen for the procedure would be 1,239. (In numerology, you will remember, James, this number symbolizes "being on the right path to achieve the soul's mission, spiritual awakening and enlightenment, and positive changes and progress toward goals".)

The machine held a perfect, vibrationally tuned, six-sided crystal, standing sixty-plus feet high, which, once activated, would spin, hovering just above the ground, with excitable speed. Considering all it was programmed to do, it seemed a very simple object, though cumbersome, heavy and yet, at the same time, quite fragile. Using their telekinesis abilities to levitate and transport unwieldy things, the GODs carefully and deftly removed the crystal from the ship and situated it in the middle of a large, flat clearing not far from the cave. Designing a structure to accommodate over a thousand participants would require much thought and precision planning, as well as more labor to erect it. Within a few days three of the GOD engineers had devised the perfect solution. Stacked vertically ten feet above one another, six levels of clear, toroidal platforms, each encircling the crystal, were constructed. With the exception of the first or lower level, which had a total of nine circular sections, each platform included ten sections, arranged around the periphery of the platform, similar to flower petals. Each of the sections would provide comfortable seating for one volunteer and twenty Humans. Further, the design ensured that each section be exactly the same distance from the powerful mechanism. The supervising GOD would stand behind the console, a good distance from the base of the structure, and with hands poised just above the remote crystal control, be solely responsible for the entire process.

    The participants were gathered and taken to the location near the secret cave where the mechanism had been assembled. Electrode-lined headbands held firmly against skulls and intravenous, electronic stents inserted into arms were attached to all participants, after which each participant was levitated to his or her designated platform and designated seat. Seats were of a warm, form-fitting protoplasmic gel-like material to both ensure comfort and to restrain any movement.

    The Humans were understandably nervous. Nothing so foreign as this mechanical contrivance had ever been seen before. With a few treats and words of assurance from their teachers, the fearful primates calmed and followed instructions. To be fair, even the volunteer GODs were a bit leery since this would be the very first use of the highly sensitive apparatus. The participants were made to feel as stress-free as possible.

All the electrodes on each head, in each section on each platform were then calibrated to wirelessly respond to the giant crystal. This procedure would exchange pertinent and educational memories, stimulate spirituality and enhance communication between the two species. Next, tubing was attached to the stents in the arms and run between the volunteers and their Humans. Through these tubes blood, carrying DNA, would be transferred from GODs to Humans, a process meant to trigger evolution in both body and mind. An aerial view of one of the platforms might resemble a schematic of a rare botanical or marine life form.

The GODs knew this procedure could cause culture shock to a lower species, but they reasoned that since the Earthlings really hadn't advanced far enough to reasonably call their groupings "culture" there was little chance they would be adversely affected. The biggest fear came from considering the possibility of the machine overriding the programming input and perhaps delivering more data one direction than the other. The volunteers were to receive, via the memory program, just enough from the Humans' memories for them to understand these backward, lowly creatures and to learn what was needed to bring them up to the certain point in evolution where that process would be jump-started and not need further assistance from the volunteers. The Humans, on the other side, would receive not only some of the GODs' DNA, which would ensure continued evolution in an accelerated time frame, but also some of the GODs' memories which would give inspiration, insight and the recognition of spirit heretofore never considered by the Humans—all of this to ensure a natural transition into the future. It was a unanimous decision that this undertaking was essential and therefore worth the risk. This procedure, as long as everything worked as planned, would also give the Earthlings, among other things, the gifts of language, technology appropriate to their level of understanding, and, extremely importantly, open minds—to let them think for themselves and not be subservient to any perceived master. They would stand up for themselves, take responsibility for their lives—neither crediting nor blaming some unseen force for their fortunes or misfortunes. They would no longer fight each other for the privilege to grovel for treats. And, they would gain an understanding of and appreciation for their connection to all things. Instead of a limiting "*world* view" of their lives, they would now sense a "*cosmic* view."

The supervisor energized the activation command. The giant crystal began to spin. All fifty-nine volunteers and the single supervising scientist, the female GOD who had been chosen to lead this delicate operation because she was particularly skilled in choosing just the right memories to be taken from the volunteers and given to the subjects, all held their breaths. Hours went by. The supervisor monitored the mechanism and everyone involved very carefully and everything seemed to be running smoothly. All transfers were working properly. Suddenly, something went terribly wrong. Deactivate! Deactivate! The crystal came to a halt. All participants were released and levitated back to ground level.

Too late, her computers had advised the supervisor that the mechanism had been placed too close to the force field of the cave, the force had been too powerful and no doubt irreversible damage had been done. What kind of damage and to what extent would be discerned only after extensive tests were made on all participants—the GODs as well as the Humans.

A recovery period of several months went by and little damage was outwardly noticeable. Then glitches began to be seen in the brain scans of the volunteers, nothing glaring, but worrisome nonetheless. A few months more and the truth began to surface. The volunteer scientists began losing their ability to speak. They could only produce woofs, barks or howls. Obviously, the memory exchange had affected their language skills. Also, they began to exhibit shortening tails and could no longer stand upright for more than a few seconds. They lost their dexterous fingers, which were replaced with rough stubby toes and unruly nails. Even their ears became smaller. Things got progressively worse as more months went by, when more undesirable traits began to show up. They began sniffing each other inappropriately and mating with abandon, precisely the traits they had wanted to eliminate or lessen in the Human population. It was recognized that they would very likely forever be imprisoned in this new condition. Yet, exhibited in their eyes and communicated by telepathy as well as by their still gentle demeanor was their unwavering determination to continue, in whatever capacity and to the best of their ability, to serve, teach and aid their Human study subjects. (Why the GODs were more seriously and adversely affected than were the Humans has remained an unanswered question to this very day.)

The lone GOD thought they might be rehabilitated if she could just get them back to the home planet. Her hopes were dashed when it was discovered they suffered a much worse affliction—the manifestation, due to the force field's strong power, of a fate close to death—the penetration of highly magnetic nano-particles into their crania. How this happened was a mystery. Were the particles in the air, in the earth? No matter. It was a mystery that would not be solved or undone.

This was the saddest news of all for the chief scientist. She knew the volunteers could never return home. Their planet is an iron-based one and the magnetic attraction would be entirely too strong for the volunteers to resist. They would doubtless be drawn out of the ship, perhaps even before it could land and be slammed into the ground headfirst, killing them instantly! (I will insert here that this is the same reason that the type and age of the specimen you unearthed, if discovered anywhere near a modern-day landfill, will sometimes be found attached to a metal object such as a kitchen appliance.) So, these heroes were sentenced to living out their lives on planet Earth. The only saving grace was that they still had their telepathic skills intact and if evolution would cooperate, perhaps they could one day teach Earthlings that they, too, have the capability to communicate in this fashion. Interestingly, it was through telepathic communication (I'm sure the volunteers would be pleased to know!) that I learned the deadly magnetic particles eventually disappeared from the volunteers' physical makeup circa six to eight thousand years ago.

On the flip side, the Humans benefited from the procedure, even though much of their DNA and brutish memories held fast. The supervising GOD knew that while it was not a complete failure, the Earthlings, if natural evolution couldn't prove to be enough in the ensuing centuries, would have to rely on some other intervention in the future—perhaps another G.O.D. expedition—to bring them to the level of consciousness hoped for by this one. There was nothing more she could do at this point, especially since she had essentially lost all her crew members. They were no longer able to fully function as scientists. To continue their good deeds, they would forevermore have to rely on whatever retained knowledge had not been damaged by the transfer and, of course, on instinct. Fortunately, their instincts were strong. Even damaged, they were still light years ahead of the Humans.

Decades more went by, the GOD did what she could to remedy the situation, but it was futile.

As stated, the Humans did gain from the transfer: they learned to build simple structures, they learned to farm, they learned to make beer and, amazingly, they learned language. Unfortunately, because too much of their original DNA remained unaltered and their minds remained closed, their use of verbal language became noise and the noise became louder and louder. They continued to

breed uncontrollably. Overpopulation led to the formation of packs or tribes, which led to competition, which led to greed, which led to envy, which led to hatred, which led to religion and politics and, of course, wars. All this went back and forth, round and round, in never-ending circles.

Their simplest form of religion was based on worshiping the GOD. After all, she was much more powerful than the Humans; she and her colleagues had come from the sky; their technology was far beyond Human comprehension, the lone GOD and her entourage were so very enigmatic and, as far as the Humans knew, nameless. The GODs had shown they were capable of performing unimaginable feats such as cutting and transporting huge stones from the mountains, simply by thinking about the process. No other means were apparent. Stones were magically carried through the air and placed to form marvelous structures, which would then serve as shelters for the Humans. Water was brought up from the depths to the ground's surface to create ponds and lakes—again solely by the GODs' concentrating on the desire and necessity for such watering places—thus assuring the Humans, as well as other Earthly creatures, would not suffer thirst.

The majority of the Humans could not understand the GODs' power, but knew they would do anything to possess it. If only they had this power, they could then control their world, other Humans and other denizens in it and would demand being worshiped as Gods themselves!

What they didn't understand was that the GODs' power came from pure love—from the knowledge that everyone and everything is connected and that only when the ALL is recognized as ONE can the individual parts embrace their power. This recognition can be attained only after reaching a level of growth in mind and spirit where one "knows" the ONE, or SOURCE. Doing battle with or manipulating others in order to gain power, in fact, negates true power.

These actions only block or prolong the seeker's journey to enlightenment.

The GODs' intent was to help the Humans along this journey. The Humans had a long way to go. Only a few had an inkling—a spark—that told them there was more to life than selfishly seeking control of everything they encountered. Two of those few were a mated couple, Zech and Suzu. Zech was especially gifted in grasping the more technical concepts of the higher teachings brought to Humans by the GODs. His mate, Suzu, being more right-brained than Zech, was able to sense and appreciate the magnificent organization and exquisite beauty of Nature, as well as being able to intuit many of Nature's subtle messages. Perhaps more importantly, Suzu felt a deep realization of her relationship with, and her place in, Nature. Together these two Humans had become prized students of the supervisor. It had taken untold generations of Humans to produce the likes of Zech and Suzu and the GOD finally gave herself permission to feel some pride and to take credit for having been instrumental in Zech's and Suzu's education and growth. With heartfelt appreciation and a tear in her eye, she remembered her co-workers. Without their friendship, hard work and invaluable input in the early years, creating the groundwork for the project, and their valiant efforts during the ill-fated (and on-going) volunteer stage, the work could not have been done—and Zech and Suzu might never have evolved. While contemplating all that had passed during all these years on planet Earth, the GOD was keenly aware that the acknowledgment of these accomplishments could not have come at a more appropriate moment.

The time was fast approaching for the GOD to depart Earth and start her trek back home. Despite all the disappointments and failure to complete the project in a favorable manner, the home planet deserved reports on the studies and explanations of all that had transpired on planet Earth. She and the volunteers had been on this planet for millennia by now. She needed to make final preparations for her flight and to make certain she would be leaving the Earthlings and her beloved comrades in as stable a situation as was possible.

(In case you're wondering why time had not aged the GODs, it is due to the fact that their home planet's orbit around the sun takes hundreds of times longer than does the Earth's, making their bodies' biological clocks slower, thereby making the GODs seemingly ageless by comparison to Humans—much as a Human seems immortal to a fly. This "immortality" or extremely long lifetime was eventually lost in the later generations of volunteers, who, having been born on Earth, became adapted to its cycles. Now they live what we consider normal life spans.)

Backing up a bit here, I want to give you a better description of what transpired fairly soon after the participants in the transfer/exchange procedure were released from the laboratory. Suffice it to say, the Humans who had not been selected for the procedure had long before spread over the globe, living in their pre-GOD primitive ways, proliferating like maggots with only the faintest memories of their encounter with the higher beings.

Of the 1,180 chosen Humans who received the Alien memory and DNA enhancement, the most enlightened two-hundred-eighty-three banded together and settled near the Hombori mountains, near what we know today as Timbuktu, in Mali, Africa, and lived in caves not too distant from the one where the lonely astronaut stayed with her spaceship. These more promising members of the Human race lived side-by-side with 50 of the hapless volunteers, creating a community of 333 members in total.

(As you know, the number "three-three-three" is a very auspicious one. It represents having merged with the ascended

Masters; magical power; a doorway to other dimensions; union of body, mind and spirit; becoming One; optimism, creativity, intuition, positivity and growth. We can be quite reasonably assured that the supervisor GOD had consulted SOURCE, then calculated the numbers for the formation of this important group of Humans and their ever-generous and loving alien teachers.)

For years things were peaceful and it looked as though this group of Humans might, due to its finally acknowledging and accepting the intelligence and guidance of the volunteers, actually grow and begin thinking for themselves! They might truly attain the level of consciousness the GODs had so hoped to bestow on them.

The other transfer/enhanced 897, in spite of the attempts by the nine volunteers who, out of ingrained loyalty to duty, had followed their Humans into other parts of the globe and stayed with them to encourage more advanced behavior, reverted to many of their churlish and vulgar ways. Chances are not unlikely that at least some of the nine GODs who could no longer control the beasts, met, eventually, with unhappy ends. And we have no way of knowing whether or not any of their earlier good influences ever resurfaced in themselves or their students. This group had scattered to great distances. Fortunately, their far-flung travels rendered them harmless and unable to deliver any negative influence on the 333 tribe.

The 283 Humans of the 333 tribe worked at being loving and respectful of the now seemingly somewhat-lesser GODs, taking good care of them, even giving them treats as they remembered having received when their roles were reversed. The GODs graciously accepted their diminished roles, knowing that, in fact, they still were far more advanced, especially spiritually, than the Humans, even though physically they were no longer as agile or dexterous. The Humans, unaware they were still receiving lessons telepathically from their volunteers, worked at improving the loftier parts of their intellect, realizing that if they succumbed to the lower they would never reach the aspired-to level of the GODs, whom they so desperately wanted to emulate. Telepathic messages convinced them to use common sense when considering progeny—bringing forth children only when and if it made sense when considering all parts of the whole: the entire community as well as the entire planet. The same was practiced by the volunteers.

Over the eons since they had arrived on Earth and endured the DNA transfer with the Humans, the GODs' original mission had blurred somewhat. It was as if they were essentially newly created beings, and as such they heeded Nature's call and were now free to procreate. Still, they remembered the power and responsibility. These soon-to-be stranded, cranial-damaged, yet mentally keen and remarkably cheerful volunteers continued to enjoy living with and observing this group of Earthlings and took pride in knowing they had had a hand, or paw, in the many positive changes seen in the thought processes of these creatures. (It may interest you to know, by the way, since your specimen is so much smaller than an original GOD would have been, that until recently most of the volunteers' offspring decreased in size somewhat with each new generation. We now see in our world all shapes and sizes in their descendants.)

The 283 learned language and used it to benefit the tribe. With aid from the fifty volunteers and the supervisor they learned to read and write, too. Although now physically limited, the volunteers were able to scratch reasonably accurate letters in the dirt and form words; then, with their tails or noses, point to the objects, which the words spelled. It was a slow process, but it worked and the Humans got a rudimentary knowledge of reading and writing. The big difficulty was in vocalizing the words. This is where the supervisor came in. She taught them to sound out the letters, just as we teach children today. That's all she could do for them. She needed to be on her way. She felt they would be all right and that the language skills would improve over time at their own pace. At least, she was pleased to note, this group had the drive to continue learning. And, with Zech and Suzu setting the example, she knew they would rise to the occasion.

She couldn't be as optimistic about the other 897!

Trouble was brewing in the outer territories. The 897, who had loosely formed separate tribes, were unable to live in harmony with each other, with other creatures or with Mother Earth. Even though their number also bode positivity, because these Humans were spiritually deficient and unaware of spiritual and cosmic influences, they had no idea how to embrace that positivity and benefit from it. They continued to overpopulate at an astounding rate, and they took advantage and misused one of the Alien memories they received during the transfer on how to produce beer and other alcoholic beverages. (Another bit of history, James, which matches evidence found at your archaeological site.) Sadly, the nine volunteers who stayed with them, we can extrapolate, were probably dragged down to their Humans' level, humiliated and, I would imagine, most turned into alcoholics. These nine bred and brought into the world deformed and brain-damaged offspring (one of which is no doubt your specimen). No one was happy in these tribes. Moreover, they were angry. And envious. They were angry to learn of the 333 group's apparent good life. So, the unhappy tribes elected their greediest and cleverest member to infiltrate the 333 camp and learn its secrets. If they could just steal the elusive "power" then they, too, would be happy.

Returning to our story, the last astronaut was counting down for lift-off. She looked out a porthole of the ship and saw the 333 group gathering there to bid her farewell. It was an emotional moment for all concerned. Not only would she miss her project and her companions, but she realized, with remorse,

that she had never explained to a single Human who she was or where she came from and now it was too late! Well, perhaps they would someday learn the story telepathically.

However, as it would come to pass, the Humans viewed her departure slightly differently. Although they were greatly saddened by the prospect of never seeing her again, thanks to two brave and bright members of their family, they were able to view the departure as just the opposite from what the GOD was regretting and bemoaning. Revealing who she was would ultimately surface, and in a most spectacular way—a way that seemed to prove and guarantee that hers and her companions' work had not been in vain. The Humans' problem-solving capabilities had, indeed, improved quite remarkably.

Just before lift-off the crowd cautiously neared the cave. They had been warned to stand back lest they be injured by the exiting ship. They all heeded this warning—all but Zech and Suzu. The couple crept as close to the entrance as they dared and peered into the cave. They could not see the ship but they could see the pool of water over which the ship was hovering. Before the anti-gravity propulsion mechanisms were engaged, sending the ship skyward, Zech and Suzu glimpsed the pool of water. In it they saw the reflection of the ship. Zech hurriedly scratched in the dirt the symbols he saw in the reflection, then he and Suzu hurried away from the cave's mouth in order to witness, from a safe distance, the ship's ascent through the top of the mountain and on to the stars!

When the ship was out of sight and tears were wiped from eyes, Zech and Suzu returned to the cave entrance. Zech looked at what he had copied from the reflection and was confused. He knew the three symbols were letters but he couldn't recognize the two flanking the middle one. Suzu looked at them and immediately realized they were drawn backwards (just as the mirrored image

would have appeared in the water). She redrew the two puzzling letters, turning them to face the right direction. They both knew they had learned these letters and how to make words with them. And here was a word already made. And it must be the name of their teacher! First, D, then O, and then G. So that's who she was! Now they knew the name of the gentle souls who deserved their gratitude. DOG! And now DOG was gone! *DOG. Gone.* Immediately, they named themselves in the astronauts' honor, the Dogon Tribe (later pronounced doe-gon) and vowed to learn as much as they could about DOG. And, obviously, they now knew to henceforth refer to their loyal volunteer companions as DOGs. (This designation has persisted to this day, although we, for rather self-righteous reasons, write the word using lower-case letters.) Over time they learned the space travelers had come from, by twist of fate, what we modern Humans call the "dog star" or Sirius star system, in the Canis Major or "greater dog" constellation.

Although the DOGs (the astronauts) weren't pleased by the fact that Humans insisted on inventing religions, the one created by the Dogon comes closest to the truth, which says that Human spiritualism is connected to Human and Alien DNA, which is connected to the Earth herself. It is from the present-day Dogon people that we get some of the oral history I've shared here. Interestingly, modern-day scientists have continued to be perplexed by how and why the Dogon people knew about distant planets and stars long before we did. They had knowledge of Sirius B, the white dwarf companion of Sirius A. Sirius B is invisible to the naked eye and no photo of it was obtained until 1970! We only first suspected its existence in 1844. The Dogon were also aware that Saturn has rings and that Jupiter has four major moons.

One mustn't forget the undeniable link between Egyptian dog myths and those of the Dogon. In addition, though I won't go into detail here, it is common knowledge in our circles that dog

mythologies exist in several cultures all around the world. I'm certain, as you are a most learned scholar, that you, James, are schooled in the following:

Greece: Anubis, the dog-headed god of the dead. Both the Greeks and the Romans associated Anubis with Sirius in the sky and Cerberus in Hades.

Egypt: Anubis, male, a good, protective deity portrayed with the color black, symbolizing regeneration and the Nile's fertile soil; believed to act as companion and guide to humans in the afterlife; able to manipulate energy (perhaps lifting and transporting massive stones, etc.?), projecting it from its body as beams and able to grant powers to living and non-living objects. Could also teleport across realms. Credited with inventing the mummification process, enabling mortals to live on in the afterlife. With the moon god Thoth, Anubis weighed the hearts of the dead on the scales of justice in the underworld, judging the merits of their souls. Anpu or Anput, female, portrayed with the color white, said to be the sister of Anubis, also works as a guide for humans in the afterlife.

Rome: Romulus and Remus, suckled at birth by a wolf.

Ireland: A pack of dogs helped Nuada, the god of healing. These dogs, themselves, had healing powers they used for good.

China: Fu dogs were believed to have strong protective powers and to bring happiness.

Norway: Garm, a monstrous dog, oversees the world of the dead.

India: Two dogs accompany Yama, the lord of the dead.

Persia: Daena, the goddess who meets the souls of the dead and leads them to heaven or hell, has a dog who sniffs at the soul and tells Daena if it is good or evil.

Africa: One of the myths of the Anuak of Sudan tells of how a loyal dog helped humans gain a place on Earth and showed them how to have a long life. Another says a dog was responsible for the gift of fire to humans.

Americas: The Aztec's mythology is that the departed soul descends to the underworld after death and comes to a river guarded by a yellow dog, Xotol, the canine deity.

Dogs almost always have appeared in a positive light. That positive reputation continues to this day. We know that, over eons of time, the spread of these beings covered most of the planet Earth.

Back to the unhappy tribes' story: And so, the interloper did sneak into the 333 village, spent enough time to learn some communication skills and waited for the secrets to come his way. He was certain he was close to knowing how to claim the GODs' power and he rushed to tell the others of his group that he would soon possess "it". As destiny had prescribed, he returned to the 333 camp well after the astronaut had left. He begged for an explanation of what had happened, and the astronaut's students generously shared the tale. It is surmised that after the spy learned the whole story of the GODs and was made to fully understand the true meaning of their power, something caused a crack in his otherwise very closed mind. A light crept into that crack and he finally saw it. Something electrical caused in him an awareness he'd never experienced before. He had an epiphany! The unsuccessful thief went back to his territory realizing he now possessed a treasure, a treasure generously and freely given to him, the treasure of open-mindedness, of knowledge, a sense of destiny, a sense of connection.

Leaving the more enlightened group to travel back to his home, he was heard mumbling along the way, "DOG. Gone. DOG gone, DOG gone!" This eventually morphed into "doggone," which can still mean experiencing a sense of loss or having been damned by God. (Interestingly, and doubtlessly a part of consciousness development, the African tribe's name spelled backwards is No God.) Upon returning to his clan, he vowed to share his newfound knowledge for the betterment of them all. We don't know, of course, whether or not he was able to successfully convince his Human companions of the truth he had learned, but we would like to think that perhaps he did save the nine volunteer GODs and their poor descendants from their drunken stupors, revived their inner-GOD spirit, and allowed them to live out more productive lives. Judging from what we see today, it is doubtful that he was able to overcome the rejection expressed by most of the Human contingent of his camp. We still are confronted by large groups of Humans who prefer to wallow in close-mindedness and cruel greed.

Millennia have passed since these events took place and we Humans have become only slightly more conscious since then. Some of us, at least, have learned to recognize and appreciate the grand contributions made to us by DOG and her comrades. We embrace, both literally and figuratively, these special beings and their descendants, and because they nurtured our capacity to love, we can appreciate all of Mother Nature and her creations. Even though we now know it was merely a misinterpretation, the word DOG will always hold special meaning for us. This has been demonstrated in small part by even naming a planet after one of our cartoon dog animals—Pluto. In our dictionaries the list is long of words derivative of "dog."

The desire for power yet consumes some Humans and they are still determined to possess it through all but the proper means and for all but the correct reasons. Still unaware of what and where true power is, too many continue to seek it through organized groups

which are too often led by the most power-hungry of them all. Also, too many Humans continue to reproduce thoughtlessly. Both of these behaviors are regressive and not good for Earth or Earthlings, no matter their species. Sadly, some act just as their ancestors did eons ago, eschewing the responsibility which comes with knowledge and enlightenment, instead preferring to remain small-minded and easily manipulated by the unscrupulous.

So, in general, we Humans are still significantly spiritually deficient, but we do have a chance at expanding our consciousness, broadening our world- and cosmic-views, and gaining enlightenment. Thankfully, the descendants of the Dogon's DOG/volunteer population spread widely—even as far away as Kansas—and with the help of these ever-faithful, constant companions whom we still call dogs, we just might make it. We know, after eons of time, the spread of these beings covered most of the planet Earth and due to their greatly varied environments, their physiological characteristics varied greatly as well. We now enjoy all sizes and shapes of dogs. Outward appearances may have changed, but their innermost sense of mission, their spirituality, their intelligence, their unconditional love for us and even their humor has held strong, never wavered.

Bad behavior found in dogs comes from abuse, in one form or another, usually done by humans. Dogs in their natural state are steadfast, faithful, forthright, honest and good. Even after having been mistreated, a dog will, if given the opportunity and just a little kindness, respond with great love, forgiveness and understanding—the very traits inherent from his earliest ancestors, those astronauts from long, long ago. Some humans have reached the level of desired evolution where telepathic communication is a reality between themselves and their dog companions. Rupert Sheldrake comes to mind: a highly evolved human who has written extensively on this topic. You may want to read his work.

Don't you find it astounding, James, that these alien beings chose to travel thousands of light years to an unknown planet and, with a selfless mission in mind, discover, assist and mentor a species whose potential was also unknown? Amazingly and thoroughly committed, these beings suffered much hardship, sacrificed much, and yet their focus has never, even to this day, deviated.

The descendants of these marvelous godlike beings, who immigrated here so very long ago may yet be our salvation. They already serve us as shepherds, seeing-eyes for the blind, emotional support for the needy, as partners in the military and police. They work for us, comfort us, play with us, make us laugh, protect us. In short, they do all they can for us and they do so because, despite our many faults, they love us. Let them be our spiritual guides as well. Accept and embrace their profound wisdom. Take a moment and look into the eyes of your very own dog. He's trying his best to tell you something. His message is "Love". Be open and listen to him.

Well, my dear James, I hope I've added to your repertoire of archaeological and paleontological learnedness, and true delight and pride in knowing that you helped unearth an important connection to our distant past, most notably the origin of our best friends, dogs.

Cheerio!

Your sister,

Susan Lee Teal

Susan Lee Teal
February, 2013

Postscript:
As for Genetics Outreach and Development or GOD to God—wrestle with that etymological descent on your own!

The End

Full Disclosure

My brother _is_ a retired judge. He _does_ have time now to indulge in hobbies such as whittling amusing wooden figures, in caricature style, usually of judges, attorneys and others in the legal world—some of whom he has known or known of, others purely imaginary—all in the forms of dogs.

He _did_ instigate the tale by saying he had been inspired by my ancient alien studies and so was now calling himself an "ancient alien dog theorist". He invented the Kansas story about the tavern, the rare old bottles and the dog with its attraction to refrigerator doors. He did send a dog head, which he had carved and turned into a refrigerator magnet. He also said he trusted that I would keep this a secret.

Sorry, Jim, I just couldn't resist!

* * *

So, the fanciful little parable you've just read was contrived by me, but I can thank my brother for having posed as my muse and allowed me to have so much fun!

To the reader: If the social commentary ingredient of this story reads as a cautionary tale, so be it. I am convinced the GODs/DOGs had that in mind when they communicated this account to me.

When not gardening or doing what I can to aid animals, I am otherwise occupied with trying to deal with the depressing state of our environment, the very genuine problem of human overpopulation, the even more depressing political state of this country, which is threatening our fragile democracy, and trying to figure out why so many humans are so out of step with Nature, and by extension, the Cosmos. Oh, and I try to stay abreast of reports dealing with extraterrestrials, because, you see, fifty years ago, in Venezuela, I experienced encounters with a couple of them. Regrettably, they were not DOGs. I live with my wonderfully understanding husband, Dennis, in our lovely abode overlooking some of New Mexico's spectacular and enchanted landscape.

Susan Lee Teal
Santa Fe, New Mexico

* * *

Postscript: Jim died in 2019. Before he transitioned, he told me he liked my story.

About the author

Susan Lee Teal is an octogenarian who really hasn't grown up yet, a Kansas-born, Colorado-reared artist, designer, animal lover and globetrotter who has lived in Italy, Spain, Venezuela, Saudi Arabia and Kenya and visited many other countries. It was in South America where she had a genuine encounter with extraterrestrials. She now lives in New Mexico with her husband and they both tend to many of the wild creatures in their neighborhood. They were the long-time caretakers of a loyal dog named Panda, whose spirit has returned to live with the GODs.

Made in the USA
Monee, IL
23 May 2025